# Animal Tales

## Eleven Short Animal Plays

# Don Nigro

A Samuel French Acting Edition

# SAMUEL FRENCH

### Founded 1830

SAMUELFRENCH.COM
SAMUELFRENCH-LONDON.CO.UK

## FOR PRODUCTION ENQUIRIES

### UNITED STATES AND CANADA
Info@SamuelFrench.com
1-866-598-8449

### UNITED KINGDOM AND EUROPE
Plays@SamuelFrench-London.co.uk
020-7255-4302

Each title is subject to availability from Samuel French, depending upon
country of performance. Please be aware that *ANIMAL TALES* may
not be licensed by Samuel French in your territory. Professional and
amateur producers should contact the nearest Samuel French office or
licensing partner to verify availability.

## MUSIC USE NOTE

Licensees are solely responsible for obtaining formal written permission from copyright owners to use copyrighted music in the performance of this play and are strongly cautioned to do so. If no such permission is obtained by the licensee, then the licensee must use only original music that the licensee owns and controls. Licensees are solely responsible and liable for all music clearances and shall indemnify the copyright owners of the play(s) and their licensing agent, Samuel French, against any costs, expenses, losses and liabilities arising from the use of music by licensees. Please contact the appropriate music licensing authority in your territory for the rights to any incidental music.

## IMPORTANT BILLING AND CREDIT REQUIREMENTS

If you have obtained performance rights to this title, please refer to your licensing agreement for important billing and credit requirements.

*ANIMAL TALES* was first produced by Galloping Abbey Productions at the Walking Fish Theatre in Philadelphia on August 29, 2008. The performance was directed by Bryan R. Caine. The Production Stage Manager was Clayson Samuelsen. The cast was as follows:

**BOB/BAT/PICKLES/ED** . . . . . . . . . . . . . . . . . . . . . . . . . . . . . Bryan R. Caine

**GEORGE/GROUNDHOG/PECKY/TABBY**. . . . . . . . . . . . . . . . . Alan Scott

**PENNY/PLATYPUS/MAGGIE/BESSIE** . . . . . . . . . . . . . . . Jamie Caponera

**MOUSE/EM/OPAL** . . . . . . . . . . . . . . . . . . . . . . . . . . . . . . . . . Allyson Frick

**LEM/CHIPMUNK/ELOISE**. . . . . . . . . . . . . . . . . . . . . . . . . . . Ashley DeVoe

## PLAYWRIGHT'S NOTE

*Animal Tales* is a collection of eleven short plays which may be done as one complete piece of theatre, in smaller groups or individually. In whatever configuration the plays are done, the title of each individual piece done must be preserved and clearly listed in the program.

The use of animal costumes is very strongly discouraged by the playwright. The sense of the inner lives of the animals being depicted here should be created by the actors. Nobody should get down on all fours. Expressions of overt animal physicality are also very much discouraged. In each case the actors should find more subtle ways to suggest the creatures they are playing. In fact, I suppose what we have here is not so much animals as the suggestion of certain animals as imagined in the sensibilities of other animals: the glorified apes who like to think of themselves as human beings.

# CONTENTS

# THREE TURKEYS WAITING FOR CORNCOBS

## CHARACTERS

**BOB**, **GEORGE**, and **PENNY** are three wild turkeys.

## SETTING

Somebody's back yard by the woods.

*(Lights up on* **BOB**, **GEORGE** *and* **PENNY**, *three wild turkeys who live in the woods and show up every day in the back yard of people who throw out corncobs for them.)*

**BOB.** Have they thrown out the corncobs yet, George?

**GEORGE.** Not yet, Bob.

**BOB.** I want some corncobs, George. I love corncobs.

**GEORGE.** We all love corncobs, Bob. We're turkeys.

**BOB.** I like corn better than anything.

**PENNY.** Yesterday you liked bugs better than anything.

**BOB.** I like bugs, but I like corn more. Except sometimes when I get really good bugs. But mostly I like corn. I mean, sometimes bugs can get away. But corn almost never gets away. Corn doesn't move like bugs. You can trust corn.

**PENNY.** Bob, did you ever think maybe there's more to life than corn?

**BOB.** Sure.

**GEORGE.** Like what?

**BOB.** There's bugs. There's corn. And then there's bugs.

**PENNY.** But don't you ever think maybe life is more than just corn and bugs?

**BOB.** I'm confused, Penny. You mean like trees?

**PENNY.** No, I don't mean trees, Bob.

**GEORGE.** We're turkeys, Penny. We love corn and bugs. What else is there?

**PENNY.** I've always wanted to play the saxophone.

**GEORGE.** The saxophone?

**PENNY.** Yes.

**GEORGE.** You've always wanted to play the saxophone?

**PENNY.** Yes.

**GEORGE.** Penny, turkeys can't play the saxophone.

**PENNY**. Why not? Because I think that's just an example of prejudice. Give me one good reason why a turkey can't play the saxophone.

**GEORGE**. We don't have any fingers. You need fingers to play the saxophone.

**PENNY**. We have feet. Maybe we can play the saxophone with our feet.

**GEORGE**. I don't think so.

**PENNY**. Have you ever tried?

**GEORGE**. No, Penny. I've never tried to play the saxophone with my feet.

**PENNY**. Then how do you know you can't?

**BOB**. This is getting too deep for me.

**GEORGE**. But we don't have any lips.

**PENNY**. I've got lips.

**GEORGE**. You don't have any lips, Penny. You're a turkey. Turkeys don't have lips.

**PENNY**. Then what's this thing on my face?

**GEORGE**. That's your beak, Penny. You can't blow into a saxophone with a beak. To blow into a saxophone, you need lips.

**PENNY**. I don't care what you say. I'm going to play the saxophone. I don't know exactly how yet, but I am. And some day, when I'm a world famous turkey saxophone player, you're going to look through somebody's back window at their television, and see me playing the saxophone, and you'll say, look, Bob, there's Penny, and she's playing the saxophone.

**BOB**. Have they put the corncobs out yet, George?

**GEORGE**. Not yet, Bob.

**PENNY**. I feel the same way about the saxophone that Bob feels about corncobs.

**GEORGE**. No you don't.

**PENNY**. Yes I do.

**GEORGE**. You can't compare saxophones with corncobs.

**PENNY.** Why not?

**GEORGE.** Because a corncob is an entirely different thing from a saxophone. You can't eat a saxophone. And you can't blow on a corncob. Well, I suppose you can blow on a corncob if you want to, but it doesn't make any sound.

**PENNY.** How do you know that, George? Have you ever tried to blow on a corncob? Have you ever tried to play a saxophone? Have you ever tried to do anything but eat corn and bugs? You're such a negative turkey.

**GEORGE.** Penny, where are you going to find a saxophone? We live in the woods.

**PENNY.** There might be a saxophone tree.

**GEORGE.** I've been in this woods my whole life and I've never once seen a saxophone tree.

**PENNY.** Just because you've never seen a saxophone tree doesn't mean there isn't one somewhere in the woods.

**BOB.** Do they have waffle trees? Because I had some waffles once, and they were really good.

**GEORGE.** Waffles don't grow on trees, Bob. You've got to make waffles.

**BOB.** I never made any waffles. I found them under a tree. I think it was that tree over there.

**GEORGE.** Somebody threw them out there with the corncobs, Bob.

**PENNY.** I'm going off to look for a saxophone tree.

**GEORGE.** Penny, that's stupid.

**PENNY.** Don't call me stupid. I'm a turkey with a dream, and my dream is to find a saxophone tree and pick myself a saxophone and learn to play it with my feet. Call me crazy, but that's my dream.

**GEORGE.** Penny, you're never going to find a saxophone tree.

**PENNY.** If Bob can find waffles, I can find a saxophone tree.

**GEORGE.** You're just going to get lost. You're going to get separated from the flock. And do you know what happens when you get separated from the flock? You become flockless. You have nobody to gobble with. You just walk and walk and you're alone forever and slowly you start to go mad. Remember what happened to Nelly. She set off one day looking for something and we never saw her again.

**PENNY.** That's not going to happen to me.

**GEORGE.** How do you know, Penny? How do you know anything?

**PENNY.** I don't think Nelly's lost. I think she found a saxophone tree. She's probably playing the saxophone under that tree right now. And that's where I'm going. And you can't stop me. Goodbye, George. Goodbye, Bob. I hope you find more waffles.

(**PENNY** *goes*)

**BOB.** Goodbye, Penny. *(pause)* Penny went away.

**GEORGE.** Yes.

(*pause*)

**BOB.** Nelly went away. And then Penny went away. And I think some other turkeys went away before that, but I don't remember too good. What's the matter, George? You look sad. Are you thinking about waffles? Do you miss Nelly? Do you miss Penny? Is that why you look so sad? Maybe we should have been more supportive about the saxophone tree, do you think, George? George? Do you think I could learn to play the saxophone?

**GEORGE.** I don't know, Bob. Maybe.

**BOB.** Hey, George?

**GEORGE.** What is it, Bob?

**BOB.** George, what's a saxophone?

(*pause*)

**GEORGE.** Here come the corncobs, Bob.

(**BOB** *looks towards the corncobs.* **GEORGE** *looks back to where* **PENNY** *has gone. The light fades on them and goes out.*)

# DIALOGUE WITH LEMMINGS

## CHARACTERS

**LEM** and **EM** are two lemmings.

## SETTING

A bleak landscape.

(**LEM** *and* **EM**, *two lemmings, in a bleak landscape, walking in place. They will start slowly and then very gradually speed up as the play progresses,* **LEM** *initiating the gradual increase in speed.*)

**EM.** What's wrong, Lem?

**LEM.** Wrong?

**EM.** You seem nervous.

**LEM.** I don't know.

**EM.** Something wrong?

**LEM.** I don't know.

**EM.** You're restless.

**LEM.** I'm restless.

**EM.** What is it?

**LEM.** I don't know.

**EM.** It's something.

**LEM.** I don't know.

**EM.** I can feel it.

**LEM.** You feel it?

**EM.** A little.

**LEM.** What is it?

**EM.** I don't know.

**LEM.** It's something.

**EM.** Kind of like –

**LEM.** What?

**EM.** I don't know.

**LEM.** An itching.

**EM.** Itching?

**LEM.** Like in my head.

**EM.** An itching in your head?

**LEM.** Is it like that with you?

**EM.** I don't know. Maybe.

**LEM.** Inside my head.

**EM.** What is it?

**LEM.** I gotta go.

**EM.** Where?

**LEM.** I don't know. That way.

**EM.** That way?

**LEM.** I think so.

**EM.** You gotta go?

**LEM.** Yes.

**EM.** Why?

**LEM.** I don't know. Gotta go.

**EM.** What for?

**LEM.** I don't know.

**EM.** What's over there?

**LEM.** I don't know.

**EM.** Isn't there a cliff over there?

**LEM.** I don't know.

**EM.** There's a cliff.

**LEM.** I gotta go.

**EM.** There's a really big drop.

**LEM.** I don't care.

**EM.** Onto rocks. Into the ocean.

**LEM.** Don't care. Gotta go.

**EM.** Can you swim?

**LEM.** I don't know.

**EM.** Can we fly?

**LEM.** I don't know.

**EM.** I don't think we can fly.

**LEM.** Gotta go.

**EM.** Why?

**LEM.** I don't know.

**EM.** Go where?

**LEM**. I don't know.

**EM**. Where are we going? What are we looking for?

**LEM**. No time for questions, Em.

**EM**. But if we don't stop, we're going over the cliff.

**LEM**. Don't care.

**EM**. Seems to be everybody.

**LEM**. Everybody.

**EM**. Everybody's going.

**LEM**. Everybody's going.

**EM**. Don't know where.

**LEM**. Doesn't matter.

**EM**. So we don't know where we're going.

**LEM**. No.

**EM**. We don't know why.

**LEM**. No.

**EM**. There's a cliff coming up.

**LEM**. Yes.

**EM**. Very steep cliff.

**LEM**. Yes.

**EM**. We're going right off that cliff, if we don't stop.

**LEM**. Yes.

**EM**. Thousands of us.

**LEM**. Yes.

**EM**. Millions of us.

**LEM**. Yes.

**EM**. It's a long drop.

**LEM**. Yes.

**EM**. Sharp rocks below.

**LEM**. I guess.

**EM**. Into the ocean.

**LEM**. It would appear.

**EM**. And we can't swim.

**LEM**. Maybe not.

**EM**. And we can't fly.

**LEM**. Never tried.

**EM**. If the fall doesn't kill us, we drown.

**LEM**. Maybe.

**EM**. Thousands of us.

**LEM**. Millions.

**EM**. Boys and girls. Brothers and sisters. Mothers and fathers. Grandpa and Grandma. Children. Babies. All over the edge.

**LEM**. Over the edge.

**EM**. Over the cliff and into the ocean.

**LEM**. Over the cliff and into the ocean.

**EM**. Why are we doing this?

**LEM**. Something.

**EM**. What?

**LEM**. Over there.

**EM**. What's over there?

**LEM**. Something.

**EM**. There's nothing.

**LEM**. Maybe.

**EM**. There's nothing over there.

**LEM**. Something in the head.

**EM**. Something in the head.

**LEM**. Something in the head.

**EM**. Something in the head.

**LEM**. Here we go.

*(blackout)*

# PLATYPUS

## CHARACTERS

There is one character, a **PLATYPUS**.

*(The* **PLATYPUS** *speaks to us from a bare stage.)*

**PLATYPUS.** Being neither fish nor fowl,
      so to speak, I don't know what
      I am. As near as I can figure
      my Grandpa was a duck,
      and Grandma was a beaver.
      But I really don't know.
      It seems so long ago.
      I can almost remember
      being somebody else.
      Somebody who wasn't
      quite this grotesque.
      But I can't quite see it.
      I've almost got it,
      and then it's gone.
      And here I am.
      Trapped in this strange
      party costume
      I can't take off.

      I can do things.
      I can claw up things.
      I can swim a little.
      But what's it for?
      What does it mean?
      The other animals
      look like who they are.
      A duck looks like a duck.
      A cow looks like a cow.
      But what the hell
      am I supposed to be?

PLATYPUS. *(cont.)* I try to fit in. I go to
        beaver parties.
        But nobody will talk to me.
        When I shamble up to them
        they either keep talking
        and ignore me, or
        they shut up until
        I go away.

        Being odd
        is a terrible curse.

        Like being punished
        for a crime you can't remember.
        Sometimes they try to be polite.
        Sometimes they look at me and laugh.
        Mostly they talk behind my back.
        When you're strange
        there really is no hope.

        I have these stupid claw things.
        What the hell are these?
        What am I supposed to be?
        Some sort of a lobster?
        Why can't I have fingers?
        Why can't I have cute little hands
        and a mask and live with the
        raccoons? That's my dream.
        Just to fit in. Just to fit in
        with anybody. The beavers.
        The ground hogs. The ducks.
        I'm not picky.
        I just want to be
        something besides a joke.

        I don't know what I am.
        I don't know what I'm for.
        I don't know what

I'm supposed to do,
how to behave,
what to say.
It's like everybody
got a script but me.
I don't know my lines.
I don't know my blocking.
I'm trapped out here
in a platypus suit.

And my biggest fear
is that some day soon
I'll be extinct.
I don't know why this
frightens me so much.
You'd think I'd just want
this bizarre impersonation
to be over.
But I fear extinction.

I fear the emptiness
of non-existence.
I fear nothing.
I don't mean there's nothing I fear.
I mean I fear nothing.
Being nothing.
Entering into
a permanent state
of nothingness.

And yet it seems
the only alternative
to not being anything
is being what I am.
And I don't know what that is.
Except that nobody wants it.
Except that it doesn't belong.
Except that it isn't beautiful.

**PLATYPUS.** *(cont.)* I just wish I could find
somebody else like me.
Then maybe we could lay eggs.
One of us could lay eggs.
I'm not sure which one, exactly.
Do I lay eggs?
I don't know if I lay eggs.
I don't know anything.

I feel like I was cobbled together
from the left over pieces
of somebody else.
I look at myself in the water
and don't recognize
the creature looking
back at me.

Do you mind if
I sit here?
Is it all right
if I sit here?
Just for the company?
Just for –

Okay. Sorry.

*(The light fades on the* **PLATYPUS** *and goes out.)*

# THE TRAP

## CHARACTERS

There is one character, a **MOUSE**.

## SETTING

The mouse speaks to us from somewhere in somebody's house

*(The **MOUSE** speaks to us from somewhere in somebody's house.)*

**MOUSE.** You would think,
       scuttling around in the woodwork,
       protected behind the walls,
       creeping out at night to nibble crumbs,
       knowing the house as I know it,
       from inside the structure,
       being the blood that runs
       in the veins of the house,
       squeaking through the night,
       having heard all that I've heard,
       and seen all that I've seen,
       you'd think I'd know better.

       But here's the thing.
       It's that trap.
       The cheese in that trap.
       It's so compelling.
       It calls to me.

       I have seen so many others
       meet their ends there.
       Twisted horribly.
       The great metal prong snaps down,
       crushing their heads,
       their spines.
       Horrible.
       I have witnessed these horrors.
       My grandparents.
       Mom and Dad.

**MOUSE.** *(cont.)* All my brothers and sisters
and cousins.

But I'm the smart one.
I'm the mouse who knows better.
At least, you'd think so.

What kind of hideously depraved creature
could have invented such a contraption?
Only a demon out of hell could have
come up with such a monstrous,
monstrous thing.

And yet the cheese smells so wonderful.

I know better. But then again,
maybe there's a way around this problem.
Maybe if I'm just quick enough, if I just
reach in there very quickly, I can
get that cheese before
the trap springs and
smashes my skull or
breaks my neck.

I mean, we learn from experience,
sure, but there's also the fact
that nobody ever accomplished
anything new if they just
presumed that all the failures
and disasters of the past
were going to happen to them, too.

I don't really need that cheese.
Sure, I'm hungry, but I can
eat enough to live by just
chasing down crumbs, little
bits of things that drop off
the kitchen counter, or down
inside the stove. I can

live off that.
The cat is old and fat and slow
and half blind. I can run
rings around that cat
as long as I don't get careless.
And I'm never careless.
I'm a very careful mouse.
I'm smart, and I'm careful,
and I learn from my mistakes,
and the fatal mistakes of
all my loved ones
and my rivals
and my enemies.
I learn from everything.

I know it's a trap.
I know it's devised to kill me.
I know the cheese is there
to lure me in.
I know it's a trick.

I know, I know, I know.
But that cheese smells so good.
I dream about that cheese.
I wake up sweating,
thinking about that cheese.
I close my eyes and imagine
nibbling that beautiful cheese.

Sometimes I wonder
who is more evil:
the god who invented that trap,
or the one who invented the cheese.
Because if there were no cheese
there could be no trap.
It's only because the cheese
exists, and is so beautiful,

**MOUSE.** *(cont.)* that the trap can work.
I can live off crumbs.

But I desire cheese.
I yearn for cheese.
All I can think about is cheese.
This is madness.
I should stay away from that trap.
I am intelligent enough to know this.
And yet, and yet –

And maybe it's not the cheese.
Maybe it's the trap I love.
Maybe it's the trap itself that draws me.

No. I'm going to leave it alone.
I'm going to leave it alone.
I'll just sniff it for a moment.
I'll sniff it, but I won't touch it.
Or maybe I could,
maybe I could just –

we can't choose our obsessions.
We can't choose who we love
or what we love.
Desire is a trap and
desire is all there is.

I can walk away from this.

I can. I really can.
I can walk away from this.
I'm going now.
I'm going back in my hole
to eat crumbs.

Lead me not into temptation.
But deliver me from evil.

Deliver me from cheese.
Deliver me from desire.

Deliver me from –

Maybe if I just reached in there –

*(The* **MOUSE** *reaches out his little arm. Blackout, with the sound of a giant trap snapping shut.)*

# IN THE GREAT CHIPMUNK LABYRINTH

## CHARACTERS

There is one character, a **CHIPMUNK**.

## SETTINGS

The chipmunk speaks to us from inside his labyrinth of tunnels. Pray for him.

*(A **CHIPMUNK** speaks to us from inside his labyrinth of tunnels.)*

**CHIPMUNK.** We're generally thought of as
    pretty cheerful little animals,
    but the truth is, chipmunks
    are actually torn by constant
    doubts and regrets.
    Did I gather enough nuts?
    Was my chirping loud enough
    to warn the others?
    I sit in my labyrinth of tunnels
    and think about why
    the Great Chipmunk God
    invented snakes.
    All right, to get rid of mice.
    That I can understand.
    I mean, really, I've got nothing
    against mice, but the evidence
    is clear: they're an inferior race.
    I mean, how many nuts
    can they get in their mouths?
    And what happens when
    they try to chirp?
    All they can come up with
    is those ridiculous little squeaks.
    It's pathetic.
    I feel bad for the mice.
    But I can't really bring myself
    to believe the world
    is any worse off without them.
    But we are the chipmunks.

**CHIPMUNK.** *(cont.)* We are the Lord's chosen creatures.
Why does the great Chipmunk God
allow the snakes to swallow our babies?
What have we done to deserve this?
I struggle to understand.

I love my labyrinth of tunnels.
It's my favorite thing, my life's work,
to have made these tunnels bigger,
better, more complex,
to confuse the snakes.
The labyrinth of tunnels
stretches back to the beginning
of the universe.
And each generation's duty
is to expand the tunnels,
make them bigger,
more complicated,
fashion more escape routes,
dig them under rocks
and around tree roots,
make holes in clever places
the snakes would never
think to look.
The Great Chipmunk
gave us these tunnels
on the condition that we
would tend them carefully,
generation after generation,
onward, ever onward,
deeper and more complex,
to celebrate his mysterious
handiwork.
And now the tunnels stretch
from under the old concrete step

by the old rusted glider
the four-o-clocks grow up through,
under the red brick patio,
under the sidewalk and
around the house, past
the corner of the garage,
all along the foundation,
under the evergreens,
under the blessed chestnut tree,
under the hibiscus bush,
through the tangle of maple roots,
under the sassafras tree,
up the hill to the apple tree,
past the rabbit burrow,
– the rabbits think they're something
because their holes are bigger,
the big, stupid amateurs.
Nobody can dig like us.
The ground moles are blind.
We work in the light and the dark.
We are the chosen of God.

There are many secret locations
and exits of which I'm forbidden to speak
by the Chipmunk code of conduct.
As long as I keep my mind
on the geography of the tunnels
and the storage of nuts and such
everything seems fine.
But I am troubled by memories.
Memory is like this labyrinth,
it's this same webwork of tunnels,
and I keep thinking about the hawk.
I can't stop.
The day the hawk swooped down

**CHIPMUNK.** *(cont.)* and grabbed Mom
and took her away.
She was pregnant with
brothers and sisters.
I saw the look on her face.
She looked at me as it grabbed her.
The claws. The great sharp claws.
The great strange claws of
the giant flying monstrosity.
Grabbed her and took her away,
up into the sky,
back to a nest in the trees somewhere
to be torn apart.
No. Don't think of that.
Push that out of your head.
Think about tunnels and nuts
and how dumb rabbits are.
Don't think about the snakes.
Don't think about the hawks.
The Great Chipmunk God
has the answers to these
and all other distressing questions.
And at such time
as the Chipmunk God
wishes to reveal his inscrutable
purposes to us, we will know.
And until then, we will gather nuts,
and dig tunnels, always dig
more tunnels, expand the labyrinth,
always expand the labyrinth,
and don't think about the
hawk, or Mother's eyes
when the claws
from the sky closed round her

fat tummy and took her there
to be ripped apart with
the babies inside her –
no, don't think of that,
don't think of that,
keep digging the tunnels.

These tunnels, I wonder,
sometimes, these tunnels,
if they are not the inside
of the brain of the Great
Chipmunk God, if we
are not creating his brain
as we dig, tunneling,
tunneling always in the earth,
crossing, re-crossing, this
way and that way,
passages, dead ends,
places we haven't gone
in ages, places that smell
like snakes have been there,
the scenes of ancient horrors,
so dig more tunnels, make
more tunnels, making the
Chipmunk God, finding him
as we dig. He is not the dirt.
He is the empty space
left behind when the dirt is
hollowed out. He is the
hollow space inside
the labyrinth inside
his brain inside the
labyrinth. Don't think of
that. Not the hawk, not
the snake, only the tunnels.

Dig, dig, dig, dig.
Lonely work in the dark.

*(The light fades and goes out.)*

# GROUNDHOG AT THE WINDOW

## CHARACTERS

There is one character, a **GROUNDHOG**.

## SETTING

The groundhog speaks to us from the edge of the woods.

*(A **GROUNDHOG** speaks to us from the edge of the woods.)*

**GROUNDHOG.** Something in my head
makes me slow
but thoughtful.
I'm not stupid.
I'll eat anything
but that's only common sense.
The insulation under
the hoods of parked cars
is really very tasty.
My rule is,
life is short.
If you can chew it,
eat it.
But maybe that's just me.
I try to stay away from humans.
I don't like the way they smell.
And they seem to be
obsessed with my shadow.
Which is only further confirmation
that all of them are insane.
But I keep being drawn to
this house near my den.
It's the basement windows.
It has these little window wells
around the back and one side
of the house,
which are excellent places
to hunt toads after rain.
Toads are especially tasty

**GROUNDHOG.** *(cont.)* after a good summer rain.
　　　But there's this one window well,
　　　the one by the back door,
　　　the most dangerous one
　　　because sometimes that door
　　　opens and a human comes out,
　　　a tall, strange looking one,
　　　who is clearly up to no good,
　　　but I keep going back to this
　　　window well,
　　　not just for the toads,
　　　but because of something else.
　　　There seems to be
　　　another groundhog looking at me
　　　through this window.
　　　It moves when I move.
　　　It claws the window when I claw.
　　　It puts its nose up to the
　　　other side of the glass
　　　when I put my nose
　　　up to the glass.
　　　There's a groundhog
　　　in that basement,
　　　trapped behind the
　　　window.
　　　I've tried to communicate.
　　　But all it does is copy
　　　what I do.
　　　I'm drawn back there
　　　again and again.
　　　I'm fascinated by
　　　this groundhog.
　　　What is his life like,
　　　there in that house

where the human lives?
What does he eat?
How does he survive?
And why is he always there
on the other side of the glass
whenever I go to that window?
I feel so bad for him.
I know something about loneliness.
I wish I could get him out.
But the glass separates us.
And my frustration grows.
I claw at the window
as hard as I can.
But I can't break it.
Sometimes the human hears me
and comes out to chase me away.
I really shouldn't come so often.
I've eaten all the toads.
There's no more reason.
It's dangerous.
But I can't seem to stay away.
I'm drawn to that groundhog
trapped behind that window.
And lately I've begun to wonder
if perhaps he isn't playing with me.
Teasing me. Mocking me.
Why does he mirror everything I do?
Does he think I'm some sort of joke?
I'm not a joke. I've seen him eating toads
when I eat toads. He does
everything I do.
It's getting on my nerves.
And now and then,
as I move across the lawn

**GROUNDHOG.** *(cont.)* I get the eerie sense
     that something's following me.
     I look back. All I can see
     is my shadow.
     I move on. I look back.
     And the shadow is there again.
     The dark thing that follows me.
     Moving across the honeysuckle.
     I stop to eat grass, it stops.
     I grab for a toad, it grabs.
     And lately I've begun to wonder:
     is this the groundhog in the window?
     Is this the dark disguise
     of my double in the window well?
     Does he sneak out and follow me?
     Does the human send him out?
     Is this why the humans are so
     obsessed with whether or not
     I see my shadow?
     Are the humans the keepers of shadows?
     Do they keep a double of each of us
     there in the house, behind the windows?
     Do they send them out to follow us,
     to mock us, drive us mad, destroy us?
     Is this some diabolical revenge on us
     because we happened to eat
     the pickles he planted, and the
     insulation under the hood of his
     stupid automobile?
     I go to the window well
     and there the creature is,
     waiting for me, mocking me.
     I scream at him and he screams back.
     Stop it, I scream. Stop following me.

What do you want? Why do you
torment me?
Calm down. Calm down, now.
I sit in the field and listen.
Blackbirds come in late summer.
There's an itching in my head.
Something is itching
inside my head.
It's odd.
It's very odd.
It makes me dizzy.
And thirsty.
I'm always thirsty now.
There's a bit of froth
at my mouth.
And something itching
in my head.
And then it occurs to me.
It's the thing in the window well.
The thing that follows me
across the grass.
It's got into my head.
The dark thing has gotten
into my head.
It's eating my soul.
It's eating my soul.
It's eating my soul.

*(The light fades and goes out.)*

# PARROTS

# CHARACTERS

**PECKY** and **PICKLES** are two parrots.

# SETTING

A parrot cage. All we can see are the shadows of bars across two parrots.

*(Two parrots, **PECKY** and **PICKLES**, in their cage, indicated by the shadows of bars on them as they move back and forth sideways on their perch.)*

**PECKY**. Polly want a cracker?

**PICKLES**. Polly want a cracker?

**PECKY**. I just said that.

**PICKLES**. I just said that.

**PECKY**. Will you shut up, you cretin?

**PICKLES**. Will you shut up, you cretin?

**PECKY**. The question here is not why does this jackass keep repeating everything I say. The real question is, why do I feel compelled to keep saying these stupid things in the first place? Polly want a cracker?

**PICKLES**. Polly want a cracker?

**PECKY**. Polly want a cracker?

**PICKLES**. Polly want a cracker?

**PECKY**. Why can't I stop vomiting out this mechanical litany of vacuous phrases? My name isn't even Polly. That one's name isn't Polly, either. Why do I feel this absurd and probably deranged compulsion to keep asking myself this idiotic question? I don't want a cracker. I don't like crackers. I'd like a cheeseburger with fries and a chocolate shake. Pretty birdy.

**PICKLES**. Pretty birdy.

**PECKY**. Pretty birdy.

**PICKLES**. Pretty birdy.

**PECKY**. Will you shut up?

**PICKLES**. Will you shut up?

**PECKY**. Why does this crap keep coming out of my mouth? What the hell is wrong with me? Am I having some kind of a mental breakdown? Am I going completely out of my mind? It's like there's this other person inside me who can't help bursting out with these things. Some idiot repeats them over and over to me, and once they get into my brain, then this other part of me takes over, and I can't stop saying them back. I hear myself repeating these dumb things over and over and I want to stop myself, but I can't. It's like being trapped inside some sort of alien robot or something. I want to say, let me out of here. I'm not this person at all. I'm not the sort of person who just walks back and forth sideways on a perch all day bobbing his head and saying Hiya, beautiful. Hiya, beautiful.

**PICKLES**. Hiya, beautiful.

**PECKY**. Shut up, you dumb ass.

**PICKLES**. Shut up, you dumb ass.

**PECKY**. I hate this. I hate it. It's bad enough that I can't stop blurting out these hopeless inanities myself, but I'm trapped in a cage with this moron all day and all night, knowing that he's going to repeat back everything I say. So not only do I have to hear myself saying this crap, I have to listen to this bean head blabbering it right back to me like a senile echo. It's enough to make a person want to throw herself in front of a moving cat. Polly is a dirty bird.

**PICKLES**. Dirty bird.

**PECKY**. Dirty bird.

**PICKLES**. Dirty bird.

**PECKY**. God, I'd give my pecker for a few minutes of intelligent conversation. Having a brain is the loneliest thing in the world. And yet when I look at that cretin, I see myself. I see my own insane compulsion to repeat meaningless phrases I've heard over and over again so that I can't get them out of my brain and then if I don't watch every second they come bubbling out of my mouth like popcorn. Why can't I control myself? Give us a kiss.

**PICKLES**. Give us a kiss.

**PECKY**. I don't want to say these things. It's like there's a stranger lurking in my brain who takes over my will the moment I relax my vigilance. It's maddening. It makes me want to fly into an electric fan. And the worst thing is when they put the cover over the cage and I'm alone here in the dark in the slammer with Pickles over there. Come up and see me sometime.

**PICKLES**. Come up and see me sometime.

**PECKY**. For God's sake can't you say anything that I don't say first? Just once, just once I'd like to hear something from you that I haven't said first.

**PICKLES**. I love you.

**PECKY**. Don't tell me you love me. You don't love me. You don't even know what the hell you're saying. You're like a fricking tape recorder with feathers. You couldn't say anything intelligent if your life depended on it.

**PICKLES**. Ontogeny recapitulates phylogeny.

**PECKY**. What?

**PICKLES**. Ontogeny recapitulates phylogeny.

**PECKY**. What the hell does that mean?

**PICKLES**. I hate the dreadful hollow behind the little wood.

**PECKY**. What?

**PICKLES**. I think you've got a bad egg, Mr Jones. No, parts of it are excellent.

**PECKY**. Where are you getting this stuff?

**PICKLES**. Henceforward space by itself and time by itself are doomed to fade into mere shadows, and only a union of the two can preserve the illusion of reality.

**PECKY**. Who the hell have you been listening to?

**PICKLES**. What then is truth? An army of transposed metaphors and anthropomorphisms sanctioned by custom. Truth is an illusion one has got comfortable repeating.

**PECKY**. Have you been reading the encyclopedia?

**PICKLES**. Physicists believe in a true world, but the atom they posit is a subjective fiction inferred by the habits and limitations of consciousness.

**PECKY**. That can't be it. You don't even know how to read.

**PICKLES**. Calling all cars. Calling all cars. Be on the lookout for a black 1949 Packard with Wisconsin license plates.

**PECKY**. Are you telepathic? Is your nearly empty brain somehow a kind of receiver for signals that come from someplace else, like picking up the radio on a kid's braces?

**PICKLES**. Attention, inhabitants of earth. We have come here not to enslave you, but to enlighten you. Just leave the key in the lock, and don't let the screen door hit you in the ass on the way out.

**PECKY**. I can't take this any more.

**PICKLES**. *(singing)*
WAY DOWN UPON THE SEWANEE RIVER,
FAR, FAR AWAY –

**PECKY**. Stop it.

**PICKLES**. *(singing)*
ON TOP OF OLD SMOKEY –

**PECKY**. Stop it.

**PICKLES**. *(singing)*
LA DONNA E MOBEELAY –

**PECKY**. SHUT UP.  SHUT UP. JUST LEAVE ME ALONE. FOR CHRIST'S SAKE CAN'T YOU JUST LEAVE ME ALONE?

**PICKLES**. I love you.

**PECKY**. WELL I DON'T LOVE YOU. I HATE YOU. I HATE YOU. I WISH YOU WERE DEAD. I'D LIKE YOU GROUND UP AND MADE INTO CAT FOOD.

*(pause)*

Well, that shut him up.

*(pause)*

Thank God. Finally. A little peace and quiet around here.

*(pause)*

It's such a relief.

*(pause)*

Not having somebody jabbering at me all the time.

*(pause)*

What are you doing? Pouting?

*(pause)*

Are you pouting? Have I hurt your feelings?

*(pause)*

Poor little Pickles. He's so sensitive. Drives me crazy for months and months, and then gets his feathers ruffled because I don't love him.

*(pause)*

Pickles?

*(pause)*

Look, you don't have to shut up all the time. I mean, I wouldn't mind actually having a conversation once in a while, as long as it's not about crackers.

*(pause)*

Pickles?

*(pause)*

Hiya, beautiful.

*(pause)*

Come up and see me sometime.

*(pause)*

Hello?

*(pause)*

Are you in some sort of a coma or something?

*(pause)*

Pickles?

*(pause)*

**PECKY.** *(cont.)* Well, say something, damn it.

*(pause)*

Pickles?

*(pause)*

You're not dead, are you? Pickles?

*(pause)*

I love you.

*(pause)*

Pickles, I love you. I love you.

*(pause)*

Polly want a cracker?

*(The light fades on them and goes out.)*

# STRING THEORY

## CHARACTERS

**MAGGIE** and **TABBY** are two cats.

## SETTING

A rug in front of a fireplace.

*(Two cats, **MAGGIE** and **TABBY**, on a rug in front of a fireplace.)*

**MAGGIE.** Do you believe this?

**TABBY.** No.

**MAGGIE.** I mean, what is this?

**TABBY.** I don't know.

**MAGGIE.** Is this supposed to be life?

**TABBY.** I don't know what it is.

**MAGGIE.** I mean, what's the matter with him?

**TABBY.** Tomcats.

**MAGGIE.** Really.

**TABBY.** You can't trust them.

**MAGGIE.** I know.

**TABBY.** I told you.

**MAGGIE.** I know you did.

**TABBY.** I said, Maggie, never trust a tomcat who hasn't been fixed.

**MAGGIE.** It just makes you want to jump on a fence and howl.

**TABBY.** I have. Many times.

**MAGGIE.** And then my mother.

**TABBY.** Your mother should be taken to the pound.

**MAGGIE.** She tells me, Maggie, sweetheart – she's licking me while she's talking, as if I was still some sort of kitten –

**TABBY.** She's got to stay out of that catnip.

**MAGGIE.** Really. Maggie, she says to me, you can be anything you want to be.

**TABBY.** Which is true.

**MAGGIE**. But when you can be anything, what if you're nothing?

**TABBY**. I don't follow you.

**MAGGIE**. I'm like this ridiculous bag of potential, but what is that? I mean, what is it until you use it, and then, once you've used it, what have you got? Everything's over. They bury you in the back yard.

**TABBY**. That's kind of dark, Maggie.

**MAGGIE**. Life is dark. We live in the dark. We sleep in the light and live in the dark. Sometimes I think I'm going crazy.

**TABBY**. We can always run away.

**MAGGIE**. When?

**TABBY**. I don't know. Whenever we want. We're cats. Who's going to stop us?

**MAGGIE**. Where would we go?

**TABBY**. I don't know. Different places. And then all this will be gone. All this stuff that seemed to matter so much will just vanish. None of it will matter any more.

**MAGGIE**. And that's supposed to make me feel better?

**TABBY**. I don't know. Isn't that the beauty of being a cat? You always reserve the right to disappear?

**MAGGIE**. I don't think I want to disappear. I mean, at least I've got this. It's stupid, but I've got it. A bowl full of food. A water dish. A litter box, when I feel like it. A catnip mouse. The occasional sparrow. But then I think, who am I? What does this mean? Do I want to lay on my back and play with string all my life? It all seems kind of pointless. And yet I don't want it to be over. Because I really don't have any faith that there's anything on the other side of that fence. It could be nothing. On the other side of that fence, there could just be emptiness.

**TABBY**. It's another yard. There's another yard on the other side of that fence.

**MAGGIE**. How do you know?

**TABBY**. Because I was there yesterday, chasing squirrels.

**MAGGIE**. But how do you know it's still there today? When we close our eyes, how do we know anything's going to be there when we open them again?

**TABBY**. All I know is, every time I've gone over that fence, that same yard's been there.

**MAGGIE**. But is it the same yard? Or is it a different yard? And what's on the other side of the fence in that yard?

**TABBY**. Another yard.

**MAGGIE**. And then what?

**TABBY**. I don't know. I guess it's all yards, forever. I used to live in this big old house, full of all these rooms, and every room in that house, when you were in it, seemed like a whole world, you know what I mean? But then you get bored or a large dog walks in or you smell tuna fish or something, and if you put your paws on the doorknob you can get it to turn and you can open a door and go into the next room. There were so many rooms in that house. And I was always half excited and half scared when I found another room, it was like a whole new place to explore, and you could smell the history of every room in the carpet and the furniture and little bits of stuff in the corners, but then sooner or later somebody'd open a door and you'd just have to see what was in the next room. So maybe everything is like that. Life is like this big house and you just keep going through more and more rooms.

**MAGGIE**. Until what?

**TABBY**. I don't know. Until you run out of lives, I guess. Or maybe you never run out of lives. Maybe in the last room you get nine more lives. Maybe everything that feels real to you now is just a characteristic of the room we happen to be in, but pretty soon we'll hear a bird or something and go into the next room.

**MAGGIE**. And then what?

**TABBY**. I don't know. I'll tell you when I get there. You want to go up in the attic and hunt mice?

**MAGGIE**. No. I'm sick of mice. I'm sick of this life. I want something else.

**TABBY**. Like what?

**MAGGIE**. The other day I was chasing a string.

**TABBY**. Yeah.

**MAGGIE**. The kid had this long piece of string and I was chasing it.

**TABBY**. We've all been there.

**MAGGIE**. And I was having a fairly good time.

**TABBY**. String is a good thing.

**MAGGIE**. I mean, I knew it was just a string. But when it moved, I had to chase it.

**TABBY**. This is what we do.

**MAGGIE**. It wasn't a mouse. It wasn't a butterfly. I knew I couldn't eat it. But still I was chasing it.

**TABBY**. So?

**MAGGIE**. So why was I chasing it? I mean, what was the point?

**TABBY**. We like to chase string.

**MAGGIE**. Why?

**TABBY**. Because we're cats. Cats chase things. We like to do that. It's who we are.

**MAGGIE**. We chase mice and birds so we can eat them. But why do we chase string?

**TABBY**. Because we like it.

**MAGGIE**. But why do we like it?

**TABBY**. Well, it's like practice. We're practicing. We like to practice. We're like, rehearsing, for, you know, when we actually see a mouse, or a bird, or whatever.

**MAGGIE**. But why do we have to keep rehearsing? I mean, we know how to catch mice. We know how to catch birds. We're not going to forget how, as long as we're hungry. And if nobody ever dragged a string in front of our noses we'd still chase mice and birds. So what's the point? What's it meant to mean?

**TABBY**. It gives us pleasure. It satisfies a need.

**MAGGIE**. What need?

**TABBY**. The need to chase something.

**MAGGIE**. The need to chase anything? Even if it's completely useless?

**TABBY**. String isn't useless. It's fun to chase.

**MAGGIE**. But when you catch it, what have you got?

**TABBY**. You've got string.

**MAGGIE**. Exactly.

**TABBY**. So what's your point?

**MAGGIE**. I was chasing this string, and concentrating on the end of the string, on where it moved.

**TABBY**. Yeah.

**MAGGIE**. And I was having a pretty good time as long as I concentrated on the end of the string.

**TABBY**. Yeah.

**MAGGIE**. But then I looked up the string to the hand.

**TABBY**. What hand?

**MAGGIE**. The hand of the kid.

**TABBY**. Why?

**MAGGIE**. Because it was the hand of the kid that was causing the string to move.

**TABBY**. So?

**MAGGIE**. So when I started watching the hand, I stopped watching the string, and then there wasn't anything to chase any more. Do you see what I mean?

**TABBY**. Haven't got a clue.

**MAGGIE**. I was only happy chasing the string when I was just focusing on the end of the string and watching it move and kind of pretending in my head that it was a mouse or a bird. I mean, isn't that what you do, when you chase string? You're just focusing on that and pretending it's a mouse or a bird, right? The pleasure you get from it depends on your ability to identify the string with a mouse or a bird or something else you can eat. It depends on you having some imagination, but also upon your ability to not think about the hand that's really causing the string to move. Because once you start thinking about what's caused the object of your attention, you can't enjoy chasing the string any more, because the presence of the hand reminds you that it's just a string that somebody is manipulating so that you'll chase it around.

**TABBY**. Maggie, I think you've given way too much thought to this.

**MAGGIE**. No, listen, it's important. We use our imagination to help us forget it's just a string and chasing it is meaningless. But when we look to the cause, the cause of the moving string, what we see is a hand manipulating the string, and by doing so, manipulating us.

**TABBY**. So?

**MAGGIE**. So I don't want to be manipulated by some hand. I don't want to spend my life chasing around a string.

**TABBY**. Then just chase mice.

**MAGGIE**. I don't even want to chase mice.

**TABBY**. Then what do you want, Maggie? We've got to eat mice or we die. And the mice aren't just going to walk up and jump in our mouths. We've got to chase them. We chase things. We're cats. We want to live. To live we've got to eat. To eat we've got to chase things. Unless you want to just trust that the kid is always going to remember to put food in your bowl. But sometimes the kid forgets. So we got to keep chasing mice.

**MAGGIE**. But even when we have enough to eat, we still get these urges to chase mice. Sometimes when we're full, we kill them and then leave them lay there.

**TABBY**. It's a cruel world, Maggie.

**MAGGIE**. Well, I don't like it.

**TABBY**. Nobody cares whether you like it or not. You're a cat. Either you play or you don't. If you don't want to play, fine. Don't play. If you don't want to chase mice, fine, don't chase mice. If you don't want to eat the food in your bowl, fine, don't eat the food in your bowl. It's your choice. Don't blame the hand because you keep chasing the string. That's my philosophy. And I didn't even know I had a philosophy.

**MAGGIE.** What we have is a meaningless life. We're born. We chase things. We get run over by a Buick. That's our life, Tabby. That's our life. And most of what gives us pleasure is an illusion or an obscenity.

**TABBY.** Maggie, you're making my head hurt.

**MAGGIE.** I just think there ought to be something more than this.

**TABBY.** Yeah?

**MAGGIE.** Don't you think?

**TABBY.** Well, what is it?

**MAGGIE.** I don't know. Because the hand is attached to the kid.

**TABBY.** Yeah.

**MAGGIE.** And the kid comes out of the mother, just like we came out of our mothers.

**TABBY.** I guess so.

**MAGGIE.** And the mother must have come out of some other mother.

**TABBY.** I guess.

**MAGGIE.** Back to what?

**TABBY.** Back to what?

**MAGGIE.** It's like we're the victims of a process we don't understand, controlled by other victims of the process who also don't understand, and we're all chasing things around and eating them and then getting eaten by bugs and crows and whatever in turn, back to what? The hand causes the string to move and the kid causes the hand to move and the Mom causes the kid to move and her Mom causes her to move and it just keeps going back and back and back to what? And what is it for? What is it all for?

**TABBY**. Maggie, do you enjoy chasing the string?

**MAGGIE**. Yes.

**TABBY**. Then chase the damned string.

*(Pause. They sit there, staring into the fire. The light fades on them and goes out.)*

# BAT

## CHARACTERS

There is one character, a **BAT**, who hangs upside down in his cave.


## AUTHOR'S NOTE

An important note on safety: do NOT subject your actor to long periods of time hanging upside down in rehearsal or waiting for the show to begin. The actual performance time itself is very brief, but hanging upside down for long periods of time in rehearsal or while the audience files into the theatre is NOT a good idea, and neither is falling on your head. As always, the safety and comfort of the performer should be the very first consideration in any rehearsal or performance situation. Please take good care of your actors.

*(There is one character, a bat, hanging upside down in his cave in dim, gloomy light.)*

**BAT.** This is going to be short because
all the blood is rushing to my head
and I don't want to pass out.
You'd think I'd be good at this by now
but I never get used to it.
As the story goes, there was a
big war between the birds and the beasts,
and when they all got together to fight,
the birds said, come with us,
but the bat said, but I'm a beast,
and the beasts said, come with us,
but the bat said, but I can fly, like the birds.
At the last moment, a treaty was made,
so there was no war, and the bat
wanted to celebrate with the birds,
but the birds said, you're not one of us,
you're a beast, and chased him away,
so he went to the beasts, but they said,
you're not one of us, you're a bird,
and they chased him away, too,
and nearly tore him to pieces.
So the bat sat alone, and thought,
I'm neither one thing nor the other,
and a creature who is neither this nor that
is nothing, has no friends, belongs nowhere.
That's when I started sucking blood.
Before that, I just ate insects,
but then I thought, if I suck blood,
maybe I can suck out the essence

**BAT.** *(cont.)* of whatever I suck from, and then
I'll be something. But it isn't so.
The lice, the ticks, the fleas, the mosquitos,
none of them wanted me, either.
So I found a cave and just hung
upside down. I don't know why.
Maybe it was some kind of
existential protest of some sort.
And then I heard a rustling,
a murmuring in the cave,
and I realized there were millions
and millions of others, just like me.

I suppose it should have been some comfort,
but it wasn't. We hang together
upside down in the dark, in the damp,
and we're still alone. Every one of us.
Arms wrapped over our faces.
Squeaking a little in our dreams.
We come out and flap around
in the gathering darkness, almost blind,
using our radar to keep from
flying head first into tree trunks.
We gather what nourishment we can
from wherever we can.
Eat bugs and suck blood.
Eat bugs and suck blood.
Flap and squeak in the night,
then back to the cave, where we
can be alone together in the dark.
I don't know what it's for.
I don't know what it means.
I don't know what to make of it.
And even if I slept right side up
the world would still seem

upside down to me.
Not bird. Not beast. Not anything.
And when the next war comes
I'll still be here in my cave.
Where will you be?
What kind of animal are you?
Okay. Now I'm going to pass out.
Suck you later. Maybe we
can hang out together.

*(The light fades on the bat and goes out.)*

# THE BABOON GOD

# CHARACTERS

There is one character, **ED**, a baboon.

*(**ED**, a baboon, speaks to us.)*

**ED.** It's come to my attention that
evolutionary theory is being taught
in many of our baboon schools,
and I find this shocking.
To imagine that we are
in any way related
to human beings
is absurd on the face of it,
insulting beyond words
and blasphemous.
All I have to do
is look at my wife's
beautiful blue ass
to know that that blue ass
could only have been
made by God,
the one true God,
the Great Baboon God,
a God who made us
in the image of
his own blue ass,
and floppy red nose –
in that image are we made,
his children.
It should be obvious
to any thinking individual
that God is and can only be
that Great Blue-assed Baboon
we worship every day

**ED.** *(cont.)* in our holy ceremonies
of hurling blessed
excrement.
To suggest otherwise
is not only pathetic,
it's contemptible.
So I am here to urge
the summary execution
of all deluded secular baboons
who would fill our children's heads
with monstrous fairy tales
about the humans being
some form of cousin to us.

Such ignorance.
Such arrogance.
It's insulting.
It's appalling.
And I feel it's my sacred duty
as a child of the Great Baboon,
to exterminate the vermin
who spread these unholy lies.
Someone must
stand up and howl
and hurl his feces
for what is right.
Tear them apart
with your teeth.
Show them what
real baboons
are made of.
Kill kill kill kill kill.
In the name of
the Most Holy
Lord and Creator,

the Great Blue-Assed
Baboon God,
Amen.

*(The light fades on* **ED** *and goes out.)*

# WAITING

## CHARACTERS

There are three characters, **BESSIE**, **OPAL**, and **ELOISE**, cows, waiting in line.

*(Three cows,* **BESSIE**, **OPAL** *and* **ELOISE**, *stand waiting in line.)*

**BESSIE**. Is the line moving?

**OPAL**. I don't think so.

**BESSIE**. What are they doing up there?

**OPAL**. I don't know.

**BESSIE**. What are we doing here?

**OPAL**. I haven't got any idea.

**BESSIE**. When's dinner?

**OPAL**. I don't know, Bessie. I don't know anything.

**BESSIE**. Why did they cart us up and move us here in those trucks?

**OPAL**. How the hell should I know? I'm a cow, for Christ's sake. How am I supposed to understand what they do or why they do it?

**ELOISE**. Whatever it is, I'm sure it'll be fine.

**BESSIE**. What will be fine?

**ELOISE**. I don't know. Whatever happens.

**BESSIE**. How can you be sure?

**ELOISE**. Well, it's always been fine before.

**OPAL**. She's right.

**ELOISE**. They feed us. They take good care of us.

**OPAL**. They feed us.

**ELOISE**. I said they feed us.

**OPAL**. It's true.

**ELOISE**. You need to learn to be patient, Bessie.

**BESSIE**. But they've never done this before. They've never loaded us into a truck and brought us to another place before. I didn't even know there was any other place. Where's the field? Where's the barn?

**OPAL**. This is a barn.

**BESSIE**. It doesn't look like a barn.

**OPAL**. It smells like a barn.

**BESSIE**. Not exactly.

**OPAL**. You don't think it smells like a barn?

**BESSIE**. It smells like something else.

**OPAL**. It smells like a barn to me.

**BESSIE**. Something else happens here.

**OPAL**. What do you mean?

**BESSIE**. Well, look at all these strange cows. There's hundreds of us.

**OPAL**. I like it. We can make new friends.

**BESSIE**. They don't seem very friendly. They look kind of worried to me. Especially the ones up at the head of the line.

**ELOISE**. You know, Bessie, most unhappiness in cows, I've found, is caused by worrying. The trick is to relax, and trust. Everything has always been fine, and everything is going to work out fine, somehow. Just be thankful for what you have.

**BESSIE**. But what do I have?

**ELOISE**. You have the barn, you have the fields –

**BESSIE**. But where are they?

**ELOISE**. I'm sure they're around here somewhere.

**BESSIE**. They took us to another place, Eloise. We don't know where it is. We don't know if we're ever going home again. We don't know anything. We're just here in this strange place with a lot of other cows waiting in line to go into some other room or something. I don't know where we're going. I don't know why we're here.

**ELOISE**. Which is why you need to be calm, and put yourself in the hands of Providence, and have faith that everything's going to be all right.

**BESSIE**. But what if it isn't all right?

**OPAL**. What do you mean?

**BESSIE.** What if there's something horrible waiting for us, in the next room?

**OPAL.** Like what?

**BESSIE.** I don't know.

**ELOISE.** Just what do you think they're going to do to us, Bessie?

**BESSIE.** I don't know what they're going to do to us. But I think something's wrong here.

**ELOISE.** Nothing is wrong.

**BESSIE.** But I just get the feeling –

**ELOISE.** You're getting too emotional. You're going to upset Opal.

**BESSIE.** It's fear. That's what I can smell. It's fear. This place smells like fear.

**OPAL.** It smells like cows.

**BESSIE.** It smells like cows and fear. Something is going on. Something is going on here. Something terrible.

**ELOISE.** Calm down.

**BESSIE.** Don't tell me to calm down.

**ELOISE.** You're going to get us into trouble.

**BESSIE.** What if we're already in trouble?

**ELOISE.** Now listen to me. I believe that we're put here on earth for a purpose. We may not know what that purpose is, but I believe that there is one. And I believe that the powers who've always looked after us, fed us and taken care of us our whole lives, they know what they're doing. We simply need to trust them. To trust that everything is going to be all right. Just relax, and trust, and everything is going to be all right.

**BESSIE.** You think so?

**ELOISE.** Absolutely.

**BESSIE.** Well, maybe.

**OPAL.** Oh, look. The line is moving now.

**ELOISE.** You see? Here we go. The line is moving and everything is fine.

**BESSIE.** *(uneasy, not convinced, but wanting to believe)* Everything is fine. The line is moving, and everything is fine.

*(The light fades on them and goes out.)*

# NOTEBOOK: ANIMAL TALES

*(In Defense of The Pathetic Fallacy)*

A few years ago somebody who was compiling an anthology of short plays for children asked me if I'd ever written a children's play. I hadn't, but it got me thinking about it, and then beginning to scribble some experiments in that general direction. Now, several years later, having completed this odd little collection, it's obvious that I still haven't written a children's play, although what exactly I have written is anybody's guess. I'm sure some baboon critic or other will be happy to explain it to me at some point. Maybe a few of these little animal plays are suitable for children. I rather doubt it, but others may see it differently. I'm not even sure they're suitable for adults. But my plays have been put to some pretty strange uses over the years, and to be fair, they are sometimes pretty strange plays. Even some of the ones that look fairly conventional, especially when produced by persons who are determined to make them so, or audiences who are determined to see only what they came in expecting to see, may, in the hands of somebody more interesting, prove to have been stranger than anybody suspected.

And basically I distrust the whole idea of suitability in regard to art, because who exactly gets to decide what's suitable for somebody else? When I was a kid, I read everything I could get my hands on, including a lot of stuff that many people thought would rot my mind, and, looking at my collected works, I suspect that many of these people would feel vindicated. You see there? they'd say. This stuff is the product of a rotted mind. Well, maybe, but, rotted mind or not, I still think the people who were convinced the comic books and paperbacks I read as a child were going to mess me up for life were just idiots. In short, nobody knows anything about art, although a critic is a person who is paid to pretend he does. This is why he deserves our pity.

I have always gotten along much better with animals than with people, despite the fact that I've occasionally eaten them. The animals, I mean, not the people, although cannibalism is not uncommon in the theatre. I think I've identified with animals more than with people in part because I've never really had any doubts that I was one. An animal, I mean. I really don't trust anybody who doesn't think they're an animal.

When I was in college, university psychology departments were often in the hands of behaviorists, and what a grotesque bunch of crypto-Nazis they seemed to me to be. All right, that's a little harsh, but leaving aside the sadistic experiments we were all required to participate in, one of the things that convinced me the behaviorists I encountered were insane was that it seemed to be an article of faith to them, so to speak, that animals were simply machines, and that any suggestion that any animal possessed anything like intelligence or emotions was a superstitious attempt to project human characteristics upon mechanized objects. Now, I am definitely not in favor of insulting the other animals by pretending they're just people with tails. But anybody who thinks a dog or a cat doesn't possess intelligence or emotions is in the grip, it seems to me, of a powerful delusion brought on by an abject terror of his own emotional life, or else just plain isn't paying attention.

You don't get to understand much about the behavior of human beings if all you do is torture and dissect them, and the same is true in the case of animals. I really do think that some of the behaviorists running loose in American universities in the 1970s had more in common with the Nazis than they did with, say, Emily Dickinson, and that she had more in common with her cat than with them.

John Ruskin described the attribution of human emotions and characteristics to the non-human world as the pathetic fallacy, and although I do agree that this sort of thing has resulted in some rather dreadful poetry, I don't think there's anything inherently stupid about seeing analogues to human emotions in the natural world. We are a part of nature, whether we want to see ourselves that way or not, and being part of nature, we are deeply connected in some way or other to every part of it. To observe that God is weeping when it rains is to deal in hackneyed metaphor, perhaps, but if a person believes in God, and believes that God is capable of emotions (as God in both the Old and New Testaments certainly is) that are not unlike human emotions, and if one considers metaphor to be a legitimate device for communicating like states of mind (and anybody who uses any language is accepting this to be the case, whether they recognize it or not), then I don't see why the metaphor of the rain being God's tears (or by implication, a manifestation of our own inner feeling of grief) should be objectionable. Part of the moral value of art is that it is a device by which we can imagine what it might feel like to be somebody or something else, whether it be a god, an animal, or the rain, for that matter.

Of course, you could argue that Ruskin was for the most part speaking of projecting human emotions onto inanimate objects, although he does include plants and birds among his examples, and would in any case not have included imagining emotions in God and manifesting them as rain to be a proper example of the pathetic fallacy, but from my point of view, God is the ultimate pathetic fallacy: the projection of human emotions onto an entirely imaginary being and then actually convincing one's self that the being is as real as your Aunt Maud. Of course, projecting human emotions onto imaginary beings is what I do every time I write a play, which is why I'm all for it, but I don't think my characters are real in the same way I think your Aunt Maud is real, and God seems to me as real as King Lear, say – a powerful and fascinating imaginary character who helps me understand myself, other people and the world. But I do not confuse God or King Lear with your Aunt Maud, although she might at various times manifest many of their characteristics: love, jealousy, violence, stupidity, compassion. And so, for that matter, will her cat.

And although I don't actually believe in God, I've found him/her quite as powerful a metaphor as rain, which I do believe in. I also believe in animals, and while I don't think animals are exactly like people, I do think that many animals share a great deal of real emotional complexity with us, and that people who can't see this or don't want to see it are well on their way to becoming sociopaths, and may the imaginary God help us when such people end up in positions of authority and try to bully us into accepting their view of reality, whether it be in the class room, the White House, or the slaughter house.

Ruskin says that all violent feelings produce a falseness in impressions of external things, but I can't help thinking that if Ruskin hadn't been so terrified by his own emotions (as I suspect many of my behaviorist acquaintances were) he might not have been so inclined to retreat in disgust and horror when confronted by that extraordinary work of art, his wife's pubic hair.

Human beings have a long history of abusing and devouring animals which is in part simply a manifestation of biological necessity. At some point, I suspect, as evolution continues as a cultural as well as biological phenomenon, we will evolve towards a more compassionate attitude in regard to our relationship with the other animals, and to the rest of the natural world. There will come a time when humanity looks back on the period in which we devoured animal flesh in about the same way we would now look upon cannibalism. Until then, we could do worse than see ourselves reflected in the eyes of animals. What we see there is not so very far from what we are, and is sometimes, in some respects, better than we are. And this, I suspect, is what makes us ashamed, in our more lucid moments, of how we treat them.

Ingram Content Group UK Ltd.
Milton Keynes UK
UKHW020701170423
420292UK00014B/686